A Game for
Knowledge

SENIR WONGSOKERTO

authorHOUSE®

AuthorHouse™ UK
1663 Liberty Drive
Bloomington, IN 47403 USA
www.authorhouse.co.uk
Phone: 0800.197.4150

Published by AuthorHouse 02/06/2017

ISBN: 978-1-5246-7737-4 (sc)
ISBN: 978-1-5246-7738-1 (hc)
ISBN: 978-1-5246-7739-8 (e)

Library of Congress Control Number: 2017901585

Print information available on the last page.

Introduction

David, one of the leading senior citizens of a small country in the southern hemisphere, is about to complete his mission to bring a better world to all the people who follow a certain pattern, aiming to fulfil and attain a higher understanding of man's purpose on earth.

His mission began in a small, poor, and divided country in South America. The educational system was stranded when the country was forced to become independent not through a coup d'état or by a political struggle, but by the disappointing state of the world economy.

The country was rudderless, and the various interim governments brought the country to a complete standstill. David and his group, together with the last government and those who were willing to see the country make its comeback, revived the mood of almost 70 per cent of its citizens.

They had the courage to subtly bring the country back to life. They made a practical, functional, step-by-step guide, communicating and motivating people towards a common goal of well-being.

The system was based on a complete source of information with a broad FAQ, where the people could monitor their own progress or situation in all secrecy. In times of doubt, advice and support could be given by the system. In severe situations, a personal counsellor or coach could be allocated. There was no penitentiary system in effect.

In secrecy, the system was working on a project to develop a new world on the planet Venus to ease the earth from its heavy load. This project was carried by all well-thinking humans.

Chapter 1

It is a Sunday afternoon. A fancy screen calendar on the wall giving quotes of the day stands on Sunday, 25 January. The sun stands high up in the sky, and it is almost forty degrees Celsius outside the building. The sky is clear and blue, with hardly any wind. Normally, the north or north-east wind from the sea blew over the land, bringing the temperature down to an average of thirty degrees.

It is not unusual at this point of summertime that most of the people take a siesta, an afternoon nap till six in the evening. That was when the temperature drops down to 20 degree Celsius, people come out on the street, shops, restaurants and café's open their doors.

Musicians do their tour in the city, dancing, and singing. The city comes to life after eight at night and goes one in the morning. This is from Monday through Saturday. Sunday is used as a day of meditation and for a revenir à soi.

Though today is a Sunday, for a group of people in the l'Édifice Vert, it is very intense and somewhat sad, and anxiety takes the upper hand. Even nature outside the building is standing sadly by, like the palm, coconut, and mango trees beside the lake. There are no ripples on the lake; the ducks are not making their usual quacking.

Although the temperature inside the building is constantly an agreeable sixteen to eighteen degree Celsius, people need to use their handkerchiefs to wipe the sweat from their foreheads. Tensions are high and very stressful. It is noticeable on every member's face in the room. Some of them are talking with and to themselves, gesticulating with fingers and hands.

The detecting thermometer and aura-meter, which are located on the top of every doorway and on the ceiling of every chamber, are registering elevated and oscillating body temperatures and body radiation.

The chairman isn't nervous or uneasy, and fellow members are very quiet. All of them tensely watch the screens in front of them, asking for what may come next. The members know their places and duties, and they have contacted their counterparts overseas. They say no news is good news, but in this case, they need the news, whether good or bad.

There is one thing they have no control over, and that is time. Their eyes jump from one screen to the other, searching for movement and changes on the screen. Every click or sound means something to them.

Everybody is on the watch for a sign, especially from their counterparts in Australia, but mostly from Jennifer. She has shut off her GPS communication chip, as well as her encrypted life sign signal. Also, at the border control, she is avoiding passing through DNA detection devices.

This is a good sign, especially when one feels threatened. They hope that she knows how to escape, get rid of the burden, and make it impossible for others to electronically track her movements. She has had extensive training in martial arts, camouflage, disguise, and anything useful to survive in extreme conditions. The group trusts that these arts will help her beat the odds.

The last secure message indicated that she left some two hours ago from the Australian continent, boarding an Indonesian commercial flight with an itinerary of Sydney to Manila. She was last seen in the customs hall, passing customs' secured tunnel, waving her right hand to camera one, halting under camera two, announced her name, waving her left hand to camera three, and waiting for the green light to board the Garuda airplane. The border control computer detected no anomalies in her voice, her brain's emitted frequency, and her body mass.

It is known and confirmed by shadow observers that Jennifer is being followed and stalked by three unknown, supposedly secret agents, who also got on board the same aircraft. Shadow members have tracked these three agents before and at the first check-in. They spotted these agents half a mile before the main entrance of the departure building. The agents checked in and identified themselves as British business men with offices in Hong Kong, travelling only with one briefcase to Manila. Another suspicious act is that their briefcases have been switched to similar-looking briefcases on the way after the last check-in of the airplane.

We've had a similar situation with the other five members, fellow researchers under the name R. Team 77, who came in from all the different part of the world. Especially from Mongolia and the United States, they were being followed, but this one with Jennifer looks a bit more complicated. She has been struggling for almost a week to get rid of those who spy on her.

On the one hand, the other five researchers are more experienced in shaking off their pursuers, because they were well trained and deal with this all the time. These five have the advantage of not staying too long at one site. They moved constantly from one country to another.

Escaping from and misleading one or two agents is less stressful than Jennifer's case, which is her first time facing this challenge. These agents change constantly and are more sophisticated and better equipped, so we need to address this with the board to find out the manufacturer who made the impenetrable devices they carry. We need to know the combining forces and what means of communication they are using to transmit their findings. So far the method they are using is unknown and mysterious. Who is behind this, and who will benefit from our research? Where will this fit in their project, how far is it developed, and where? Where do we have to enforce our wall to keep our project safe, and what new elements may we use as a bait to fence off these spies?

Soon we will have more updates from our shadow members, who are doing their part so that adequate measures can be taken.

Silence breaks when, suddenly in the room, one of the member shouts, "It's the 2200 news on Radio Da FM, of Bandung."

Randy, Danny, and Ronny tune in to that radio station. There is a replay of what was a live broadcast of a cockfight held on the island of Bandung. It is a very lively and agitated cock fight. The commentator, Mr Iskandar, is sometimes stressing certain words and numbers. As long as they use the Bahasa Indonesian language, it is understandable. When dialect is used in between, it becomes more difficult to understand.

Hardly anybody uses the FM frequency anymore, and that makes it more curious.

The moment is becoming very intense. We not only see the sweat on their faces, but we feel the fear and the anxiety in everybody in the room. They keep themselves as confident and fierce as possible.

"Decipher it, people – fast. Help is needed. Please make no mistake. If it is correct, in the summary section the words and numbers will be reversed."

This is said in a commanding way by David, the chairman, who wants to make sure that the people know their duty, the rules, and their codes.

It is a hour-long cockfight, and the commentator seems to be very agitated. The closing comment is very sad, but he is asking for a pause to continue after a half hour. Is this the end, or is there more to come?

The broadcasting is interrupted with some crazy gamelan music.

"I have it!" Randy shouts.

"That's it. I got it, I get it." that is Danny.

"All right... Itu bagus, or should I say, ce qui est bien." this time it's Ronny.

The three are bringing their findings together to compare and discuss. By doing so, they will be able to make their translation and their comments more realistic.

"OK, guys, here it is. 'The feather is plucked out from the chicken before flapping the wings and is safe and neatly packed, waiting to be posted by 511 to Jaka. More details will be given by Samina. Over and out.'" This is announced by Randy with a big smile on his face.

A moment of general silence follows.

David interrupts the silence by speaking in a low tone. "Hello, guys, where are we? I'm trying to be patient and be cool, trying to control my temper. Say something – I'm listening."

"Why, how, and, when? Whom to talk to?" Randy is merely probing the other members.

Eileen raises her left hand and says in a soft voice, "I've sent a message to Else in Seattle. Give me a sec."

"OK, here is Else. Her reply says, 'Give me one hour.' We will have to wait till night falls to know her observation and how she can stand by."

Randy adds hastily, "I'm contacting my friend Djida in Darwin to see what she has for me and how she can stand by."

David gives a warning sign. "People, please know that a watched pot never boils, so be careful. Eagle eyes are everywhere. Your skills, your intuition, and your determination are of capital importance."

Randy puts both hands behind his head and leans back in the chair. "OK ... Djida said, 'The bird is in the cage; body and head are at attention.' There is no further comment. This is testing our patience, people."

David tries to relax the intensity of the group. "As much I want to say relax and be at ease, I know that all eyes and ears are open. But please know that Jennifer is in good hands, and she will survive. Go home and make good use of the remaining night, because tomorrow will open itself."

The night slipped by without any sound. Nobody bothered anybody in a sense that anybody feels the need to talk to anyone. It's if there is a silence sweeping over worried and troubled waters, but they have the ability to keep it calm.

David turns to his left, which faces the window. He opens his eyes and sees daybreak, so he jumps out of bed, goes to the window, greets the sun in the east, and rushes to the room next door. The door slides open on his command with a swipe of his hand. He rushes to the screen, looks at the screen, and turns the report pages, but there are no changes that catch his eyes, no messages that attract his attention. He hesitates somewhat and then slides his finger on the left side of the screen to consult his daily agenda.

> Monday, 0900. First discussion. What's the exact reason or motivation that some people or families going on vacations to foreign countries (like the United States, Europe, and Brazil) do not return. They simply stay away without notifying their embassies abroad.

The project is called the Emigrate Challenge and will be rendered by Jameson and his three assistants, who will be tested and challenged by six heads of a mixed social and welfare commission, pertaining to the Security and Social Affairs Department.

David rushes to the bathroom and takes a cold shower. "That's cool and refreshing. I need that for today," he says softly to himself. He gets dressed with no tie and walk to the breakfast table. He pulls the second chair as if there will be someone else having breakfast with him, and he looks at the menu on the screen.

a) à la carte
b) adapted
c) full service

David puts his forefinger on à la carte. "One glass of orange juice, and one glass of still water." Then as he hesitates whether to have something else, he points to the enter button and clicks his fingers.

From the centre section of the breakfast table, a hatch swings open, and up comes two glasses, one filled with orange juice and the other with ice-cold water. "Good morning, David. Here is one glass of orange juice with a pinch of lemon, the way you like it, and a glass of plain water. Bon appetite."

Upon hearing this, he takes the glasses from the centre and places one in front of the chair he has placed by the table. He ceremoniously toasts with the non-present guest and takes a swig of his water. He evaluates his drink and says, "This is the life." Then he drinks down his glass. As he folds his left hand while staring at the empty glass, he looks at the orange juice on his right hand, holds it up, and says, "May the Gods lead your way." Then he drinks down the juice in a one gulp. He neatly places the glasses back in the centre of the table. As he is leaving the table, the glasses disappear underneath the table to be washed and put away in his private cupboard, where he has his own collection of cutlery.

As he walks down the hall, a female digital voice follows and whispers the following information. "David, your bio temperature is at 37.5 Celsius. Your heart rate is at 77. Your systolic is at 154, and your diastolic at 67. Please consider your mindset, and watch your breathing."

Upon that message, he freezes and considers the message. With resolute eyes, he looks up and pursues his purpose of the day.

Down the hall, he chooses the Blue door. The elevator takes him to the conference room, where ten people look at him as he takes his place. There are six committee members surrounding him, one project lead flanked by his two assistants, and the immediate past chairman, Frank.

The conference lead announces David as chairman of the Emigrate Challenge, at which point the cue is given for everyone to take a seat. Thereafter, the project lead commences his introduction:

"Chairman David, today is Monday, 26 January 2037. Sir Jameson will present his first of three proposition on the Emigrate Challenge, to be denoted AFGL 6045, under the heading of the Equality Challenge."

Jameson clears his throat and commences. "Sir and esteemed members of the committee, after three months of study, it is our findings that, as per the eighty-twenty rule, those few twenty seem to..."

David abruptly stands with both hands firmly on the table. He looks down at the project lead and speaks. "Look at me. Do I look like Italian to you? Are we living the Italian situation at the time of Vilfredo Pareto?"

The committee members look at David in stark shock. They are not accustomed to such a frontal attack. Their leader is a man of argument and debate, revelling in diverse opinions and approaches. Not once has an argument been shot down so fiercely.

After having said this, David relaxes his tone somewhat and proceeds. "We are with twenty-four nationalities, merging together and living side by side. We all live on equal footing, and we strive to better the welfare of the human race. We also know that humans living on this beloved planet are complex, and therein lies our challenge: to fill in the gap, take away the doubt, establish the past, smooth the present, and build the future. This is so that we may not have to live in fear and do not give the past the chance to haunt us. We can build the future with minimal, calculated risk.

"Jameson, my friend, is your study based on the rule of eighty-twenty? With the resources we have here at your disposal, have you taken into the consideration the processes, rules, and comforts provided to our people and how this impacts them? What is driving the mood swings of the rich variety of our citizens? What is moving their souls, bodies, and minds? Are they being lured, are they looking for new challenges, or are they going on an adventure tour? What are the inner urges to challenge or defy others? Is the thirst for foreign wealth so appealing or blinding? Perhaps our demand for purposeful living is too rigid. Do we have to fill unknown gaps? And how about those who left and came back after some years? What changed their mind, and can we improve the way we welcome them back? Can we also improve the way to put these experiences to students to debate this phenomenon in the classroom? Also, please note that these are the groups that leave without notifying the authorities of their intention, abstaining from two years of aid in order to establish themselves in a foreign country. Do they have relatives in those countries, and are their visions towards our culture being changed? Or are they challenging or maybe going to challenge our system after coming back? The embassies are keeping track of all the whereabouts of our members, and thus we have valuable information that is being updated daily. Enlighten me, my friend."

With his head down, Jameson replies, "Pardon, sir. I tried to fit the circumstances into the rule to cut the time, but you're right. I'm going to study it from our actual situation with their diverse characters, versus the life styles of other civilizations, in order to understand the human hunger and thirst and come up with a reasonable solution – a solution that will not and cannot be final, but it will be a starting point."

David sits back in his chair, looks to the committee members, and continues. "Jameson, Fred, Koen, and Jaime: you've understood the message. We are not here to condemn anyone, but to assist and help them to facilitate their transition. Go pave the way, and remember that time does not sit in the driver's seat."

Jameson looks at his two companions, looks to the committee members, and then directs himself to the chairman. "Thank you, sir, for the guidance. We will smooth the edges and widen the path."

David accepts Jameson's answer and closes the meeting by wishing Jameson and his team good luck. He asks nature to guide and speed the team to bring forward a good result.

Everybody is wrapping up and leaving their seats; the water and the malt drink have not been touched. David rushes back to his quarter. Jameson and his team leave the office with renewed vigour and drive to accomplish their purpose.

The social and welfare committee did not have the chance to come into the play. They sit there with their hands closed and firm on their note pads. They didn't even nod at what have been said.

This is the first of all the meetings that last no more than thirty minutes. The minute meetings have been recorded and videoed automatically, and saved via individual input in people's respective personal files.

David rushes straight to his quarters, jumps in his chair, places both feet on his desk, leans back, and places both his hands behind his head. He swings both his elbows back and forth, pointing them to the screen as if wondering, *Shall I touch this one, or that one, or that one?* He then says out loud, "Jennifer, where are you? Samina, talk to me, please." One eye is watching the doors in his hallway screen. Suddenly the purple door starts flickering, and without hesitation David pushes the purple enter button.

Randy appears. "David, word from Samina through the secure line. It says Jennifer boarded the Garuda airplane as the seventh passenger and took place at seat 33 in the rear. While other passengers are boarding after Jennifer, one passenger, the eighth after Jennifer, obstructed the passage by accidently letting other baggage fall from the luggage compartment. In this tumult, stewardess Natascha, who has the same characteristic face and posture, replaces Jennifer in seat 33, wearing the same cap and dress. The steward supervisor, Glenn, took Jennifer through the fridge door to the cargo space and in to a luggage container, taking her to the main terminal. From there, 511 flew Jennifer on his private jet to Darwin, and at 0310 a hover craft flew Jennifer to Jakarta's side gate at the Arch. We are awaiting the decision of Padma regarding the mode of transportation upon which Jennifer will be travelling to Mumbai." Randy raises his eyes from his tablet, reaches over to David, and gives him a level look. "Better?"

David turns his eyes to the left top corner of the room. He looks back to Randy and says, "What about her luggage?"

Randy nods. "Our local contact has indeed informed us that someone sprayed the luggage with a frequency-emitting electro-chemical product that can be traced by the other parties from a distance. The luggage was placed in the plane and is on its way to Manila, as scheduled.

When I asked about the contents of the bag, our man said something funny. Jen informed him that the bag consists of a couple of old clothes which she bought from a second-hand shop, old Australian newspapers and magazines, and a clown outfit complete with red afro hair and red nose."

Upon hearing this, David starts laughing. He wipes a tear away.

Randy smiles at him. "Share with me, Dave?"

David smiles back at him warmly. "Randy, to know a person is to know how she thinks and acts. These are the secrets we all carry. These actions fill me with confidence. That means that she knows what's she doing, and she is doing it her way."

Randy raises one eyebrow and asks, "So what is there to tell?"

David turns back at his screen and starts to type. He replies over his shoulder, "When you're in stress, your breathing gets irregular and laboured. In order to compensate, you give the chocolate business a reason to produce."

Initially shocked, Randy gives a snorting laugh. Then he walks away while replying, "Whatever. I have work to do."

As Randy approaches his working station, he sees an array of chocolate bars on his table and smiles. "Yeah. Know-it-all."

When the door slides close, David takes a deep breath. With his hands cradling his head, he closes his eyes and visualizes the travelling path Jennifer still needs to take. At each point he fixes his mind's eye on the features she will see, the people she will meet, and the actions she can take to make it safe home. His last image is the warm welcome Padma will give Jennifer, and he notes the similarities of Jennifer's feature with Padma's own daughter. With that reassuring good feeling, he resumes his daily tasks and heads toward to the green door.

On the other side of the premises, a beautiful glass building gleams, perched on a beautiful hillside and surrounded by neatly organized orchards of all sorts of fruit and a diverse mixture of herbs.

Upon entering the hallway, it feels like a massive greenhouse full of exotic plants and vegetables. A spiral stairway leads to a glass dome at the top, where a woman with a pince-nez resting on the arch of her nose monitors the patients, or buds as she would call them, on a large screen. She pushes her hovering stool over and turns around, where her eyes fall on David's nutritional table. "Hmm. Steak again? Right."

Earlier on, she already enhanced his water with metabolism accelerants to cope with last evening's meal. Perhaps today she should hint for a healthy vegetable dish? *Or maybe just give him a nice juicy soya burger.* She giggles to herself. She raises one finger and wags it. *Must not piss off the boss.* She types in a mild warning to be provided to him when he orders his lunch, and she provide a suggestion that she knows he will like and will benefit him. Add in a little bit of chamomile, lemon, and Stevia in his drink, and that should ease his mind till Jen returns.

She thinks of Jennifer and quickly jots down a private note on what she might be dying for when arriving home.

Anita loves her life. She is surrounded by things she adores the most: plants of all sorts. She is rewarded handsomely to take care of people. That's what she signed up for, and it's what she's always wanted.

Suddenly, her mind takes her to a dark place, where she remembers taking care of starving children, preparing and negotiating for medicine, and fighting for their lives only to see them die. That life is over now. She moved, she changed, and she is working on a solution for the whole of mankind.

A green blip on the screen catches her attention. it reads, "David – steak with salad and baked potato with sour cream." She smiles, grateful to be back in the present. *Our great leader is so predictable. May he attain the highest.*

While David is scrolling up and down the screen, he smiles and types in a group invitation for this afternoon. This is an invitation to the LAB group, Support Team A, which is manned by Randy, Eileen, Danny, and Ronny. David is scanning the files and profiling each of them. "So, what do they have in common? Let's see... What drives these people the most? Randy is an excellent go-getter. Eileen is motivational. Danny seems more to approach things analytically. Ronny is more easy going and pleasant. Good, good... We will blend this in a potion. What are the ingredients to add? OK, good. That will do it, and santé."

The invitation is set for 2000 hours. David makes sure that everybody is available unless something unpredictable pops up. In order to make good use of the time till the meeting, he scrolls through Tuesday's agenda, identifying his key focus points. The first meeting of the day is the Educational Challenge. "Hmm, let's see what possible solution might come up." He looks at the name of the project lead, and it's Freddy, a man with lots of good reputation.

The fifteen-minute warning pings on his screen for the 2000-hour meeting. *Just in time,* he thinks because he is feeling a bit peckish. After saving and backing up his work in his private disk, he make his way to the canteen.

He's the first one there, and he looks for his favourite table, which is large and circular, allowing for plenty of tapas and drinks – his kind of meeting. While resting his hands on the table, he evaluates which delicious little thing he will choose – or be allowed to choose by his lovely doctor, who is monitoring the behaviour and mood swings, especially for this last few days. *Hmm. I already had steak for lunch. I'd better take some fish nuggets.* he muses.

Before he can finish the order, his four invitees enter the canteen. Lab Support Team A rushes in upon seeing him at the table. Eileen asks, "Hi, Dave. Are we late?"

"No, not at all, I'm early – got a bit hungry and thirsty. Please join me and take your seats."

Ronny slides down in his seat and puts his hands on the table with his nose close to the screen. With a big smile, he asks, "Dave, what are we celebrating? Did we make a big win, or is it someone's birthday? Then we can celebrate accordingly! Shall we start with a whisky on the rocks with a splash of tomato juice, or a rum with lemon rings and cherry syrup?"

At this absurdity, David looks up, putting on a horrified face. Eileen steps in and places her hands on David's shoulder while sliding in the seat next to Ronny. "He's just joking. Must not have anything that will undoubtedly come back up at the end of the evening."

Danny takes his seat and advises everyone, "Based on the meeting topic and the duration of the meeting, how many tapas we should limit ourselves to, so as to not have too many leftovers?"

Randy takes the final seat. With tablet in hand, he asks, "Where are we heading, boss?"

David sits down, folds his hands, and nods at his potion in the make. "Ronny, my boy, you are not far off from the purpose of our meeting. It is my honour to toast the Lab Support A team's success of having facilitated and brought back the five researchers. This afternoon, Randy brought us the great news: the sixth researcher is in good hands and well on her way back to the base. Please order anything you feel like to toast."

The menu screen is preset by David on à la carte for meeting drinks. At this, the team scours the à la carte list for wonderful drinks. Ronny orders three drinks for three toasts, he jokes. When the last finger tip slides over the screen, the drinks emerge from the centre of the table.

David raises his glass. "This is to the successful completion of project Research 77 of the lab group. From the deepest recesses of my heart, a warm thank-you."

The team toasts heartily.

David has a smile on his face and says, "All of you are fully dedicated to support and keep this project alive. You have preached and guided everyone involved in this project. You have used the coding excellently. You have set up numerous intelligent decoys in your communications with those supporting members in Alaska, Mongolia, Australia, New Zealand, Indonesia, Philippines, India, Pakistan, Egypt, and Morocco. The five researchers – Brian, Rita, Rani, Caio, and Bo – are waiting for Jennifer to join, and they would like to express their gratitude to all of you in person."

David pauses while looking each person in the eyes. "As we all know, this is not the end of the story, but the end of phase one. Undoubtedly, the second phase will be more challenging because we are going to deal with nature and uncover the secrets it holds. We will be investigating and delving into the past to see how nature has evolved and where it is heading."

As if something magical is happening, they hear a tinkling sound of an incoming message on a secure ether-line. Five fingers simultaneously point to a pop-up screen in front of them. They check their time teller, which says 2030.

It's an incoming message from Kenya, and a big sign pops up with the portrait of Lord Baden-Powell. The message reads, "Padma says Jen OK. Leaving 0500 from Silver Beach to Kenitra – Beijos." Then the screen shuts down.

High-fives go around the table, and they toast again. Ronny says with his commanding voice, "Au boulot. Tracking time."

All of them except David retire to the observation room. Contentment is all over their faces. They hook their frequency headsets and gesture towards their screens, searching the skies to track every movement that might indicate a flight or any other means of transportation. It won't be difficult. After all, from Silver Beach at Mumbai to Kenitra in Morocco, it is some eight thousand kilometres, assuming no surprise deviations.

Meanwhile, David returns to his quarter and hooks into the screens of Brian, Rita, Irani, Caio, and Bo.

They all say, "Hi, David."

"As you already know, Jennifer is on her way to Morocco. She will land on a reserved location, a military airport in Morocco. So, don't worry – she will be joining us shortly."

"Yes, we know that. Guido and his team, Divers M, are pronto in Port de Medhiya. We are keeping an eye on the route," Caio replies.

Bo adds, "Don't worry. Our communications are secured from and through BP Central Africa."

"Thank you, guys. I am sure that all hands are on deck, and I can leave the scene with a smile. Have a good night's rest, and we'll talk soon," David replies.

He then takes a glass of plain water, drinks it, and summarizes the day. His smiling eyes indicate that all is positive, and they have learnt a lesson for future improvement.

Before turning in, David once more points to the screen, searching for Freddy, the leader of Project 25 of the Educational Challenge.

Freddy has led the project for six months; conducted 26 meetings with peers, students, and parents; and answered 256 questions concerning the educational system. This time of the year, there have been 25 per cent more young research students enrolling for the project of sustainability programming compared to last year. All of them have completed the mandatory salutations training two months ago. Rearranging research facilities and conference rooms for freshmen, as well as partnering with family members, will assist in understanding the experiences of the new challengers.

After visualizing this next day's meeting, David lays his head on the pillow and sleeps. David's left side faces the window.

When he opens his eyes and sees daybreak, he jumps out of bed, goes to the window, greets the sun, does his daily stretching exercises, and rushes to the room next door. The door slides open on his command with a swipe of his hand, and he rushes to the screen and turns the pages carefully through the screen. There are no changes, no messages that attract his special attention. He hesitates somewhat and then slides his finger on the screen to consult whether there are changes on his daily agenda.

David walks to the bathroom and takes a cold shower. He puts on a green silky tie and walks over to the breakfast table. As usual, he pulls a second chair as if there will be someone else having breakfast with him, and then he looks at the menu on the kitchen screen. "One glass of orange juice, and one glass of sparkling water. Scrambled eggs and fried bacon, please." Then he presses the enter button.

From the centre section of the table, a hatch swings open, and up comes two glasses. He takes the glasses and places one in front of the empty chair. He ceremoniously toasts with the non-present guest and takes a swig of his water. When he drinks half the juice, he has his eggs and bacon. He neatly places the glasses and the plates back in the centre of the table and leaves.

He heads to the hall, and a digital voice follows and whispers to him. "Good morning, David. You look bright and shiny today, especially with your tie on. Have a good day."

He smiles and says thanks. With resolute eyes, he looks up and pursues his purpose of the day.

Down the hall, he chooses the blue door. The elevator takes him to conference room, where nine people look at him as he takes his place. There are the six committee members surrounding him the project leader, Freddy; Ram, Freddy's assistant; and the former Chairman Frank.

The conference lead announces David as chairman of the Educational Challenge – AFGL 4000, at which point the cue is given for everyone to take their seats. The project lead commences his introduction. "Chairman David, today is Tuesday, 27 January 2037. Freddy will present his first proposition on the Sustainability Programming under the Challenge of Education."

Freddy stands up, looks to the committee, and turns his attention to David. "Good morning, Chairman David. Good morning, members of the committee. As we all know, the project of the Sustainability Programming is becoming very desirable due to the general drive, which became a wave for improving the living standard within a community, a state, and a country – and most of all, sharing this passion worldwide. It is also no small point that youngsters get to go to their countries of their choice to research and implement it, if they're chosen. The starting point is in today's need to put it in such a way that it creates a simple, promising tomorrow. The benefits of this course have hit home for not only students but also their families, who see the growth of their children's young minds and the gain for our great nation.

"Three new projects are being added to the Sustainability Programming Course."

- Reproducing and managing natural resources to satisfy human demand.
- Capturing carbon emissions, together with other waste products, and transforming them into usable, durable materials.
- Reproducing and managing resources to balance the ecological environment.

"In order to be able to realize this great success, the plan of educational challenge, and more notably appendices C to E, have been placed on the central drive for your review. They contain in short the following action plan and requirements."

- Action Plan:
    - o Because this is the first time these projects on sustainability programming are intended to go overseas, additional attachés are needed in the various countries to revise the international treaty on sustainability containing the freedom of human resource and data amendment.
        - ▪ Article V: Economic Developments
        - ▪ Article VII: Social, Cultural, and Environmental Understanding
        - ▪ Article IX: Education and Productivity
        - ▪ Article X: Reforestation and Climate Adaptation
    - o Adapted or additional campus sites with the capability of 200,000 more rooms and seats are needed. A phased 4-year approaches 50,000

rooms per phase. The expansion is based on the retention rate of students within the first year. The churn rate will indicate the requirement for more seats. Any permanent leavers will have already found alternative projects to work on.

o 30,000 rooms or seats overseas, and 170,000 rooms or seats within the country.

o 6 multi-purpose research facilities across the country.

o 6 leisure centres adjacent to the research facility.

o The existing course "From Project to Process Management to Execution in Real Time" must be adapted to fit the legal, cultural, and economic parameters of each country where the project will be effectuated.

o Full-time equivalent on contingency planning.

Freddy looks up from the screen to the assembly, evaluating the different faces. He bows his head and continues. "Upon approval, all the required analysis and budgetary considerations will be uploaded and distributed per the required media. Feedback from the watch eyes and the general public will have a review time of a month. Should any material or policy changes arise from the feedback, the next assembly will be called in the shortest time possible. In the meanwhile, final budgetary requirements in resource and currency requirements will be drafted and will also be available on the net. Mister Chairman, with this, the initial draft has come to an end. The team eagerly awaits your feedback and guidance."

David analyzes the reactions and the body language of the committee members. He says, "Freddy and Ram, thank you for your exposé. This is everything that we need for this stage in order to make the project work. We will analyze and evaluate all valuable feedback with their respective comments. Furthermore, I am sure you will be connected with the departments involved, to prepare the budget and have a preliminary financial statement of every country with which we have commercial, economic, and social ties. We will make sure that our marketing machine creates the bridge to overcome the language and cultural barriers, both internal and external."

Freddy nods. "Thank you, sir. We will make sure that all the complementary statements are attached to Project 25, and also that every correction or adaptation that may arise bears the mentioning of their respective authors."

David stands up and puts his right hand on his heart. "Friends, thank you once again. The conference lead will see that everything is taken care of, and it will be denoted as AFGL 4025. Let nature guide and speed you."

After having greeted and thanked the assembly, David leaves the conference room. In the hall, a secure screen alert catches him mid stride.

There are flickering lights. "Flash report... Flash report" appears on the screen, followed by "Operation Medhiya starts now".

David rushes to his quarters. Upon arrival, he jumps in his chair and with childish exuberance makes a dramatic mid-air point of his index finger to illuminate the screen.

An old military Arab appears on the screen, his wise eyes smiling knowingly at David. "As-salamu alaykum," Mohammed greets.

"Alaykum salamu, my friend. It has been two years, hasn't it? How is the family and the base? Are you still pulling the strings?"

Mohammed smiles. "You know I don't do that. I negotiate. And by the grace of Allah, everything is going smoothly. The family is doing OK, still the same – and hey, greetings from Caila. As you would like to know, in Diver Team SC, diver Guido fetched J from the airport, and they are on their way to Medhiya. Everything looks safe, and within a half hour they will be boarding in the sub. Know that DTSC is doing an excellent job. I'll talk to you on the other line as soon as possible. Farewell, my friend."

With his right hand on his heart, David thanks Mohammed for his sincere and kind cooperation. "Farewell. May the great Allah lead your way."

The screen turns dark, and David reclines in his chair. He transfers the wonderful message to his teams, STA and RT77. In relief, he closes his eyes for a couple of minutes and whispers into the room, "Soon, my dear."

Randy messages David. "Five hours to arrival, David. You think she'll be hungry?"

David replies, "Undoubtedly."

Randy smiles and releases the next tit bit. "Guido and his team boarded a sub using the North Equatorial current. There will be a lot to talk about at lunch. See you then. Don't be late."

David responds, "Get the team together."

At 1230, lots of feet are walking towards the purple canteen. The STA and RT77 teams are complete in the canteen, and after having hugged each other, they are standing in the hall, not talking much. They're waiting anxiously on something, not knowing what may come. The quiet is short-lived because the door slides open, and David comes in.

"Good afternoon, my friends." While everybody greets David, he pauses and looks at all the faces. "Why these dubious faces? Everything appears to run well, and there are no indications that it might end differently."

Bo jumps in. "Yes, sir. But we all are counting the hours, and as you taught us, we should expect the unexpected. That's why we're hoping we'll soon be counting the minutes, even though we are tracking the movement and see that there isn't any interference. If there was, the wall-screen would be flickering red."

David looks to the others and continues. "We also know that we all are strong in our beliefs, and that our intentions will light the way. Ralph Waldo Emerson once wrote, 'What lies behind us and what lies before us are small matters compared to what lies within us.' We all have shared our lives in a positive way with our friends and loved ones, where all of them wished to be like us. Our conscience minds and moral senses have been as pure as possible. We should not let our guards down, enabling us to continue and have our primary concern: to always think well, speak well, and act well. Are we OK with this?"

All speak in unison. "Yes, I agree."

After this, David takes his seat. The team follows suit. Some have already ordered their food, and now it's a question of confirming what they have ordered. Others are choosing it on the screen, and all of them choose à la carte. At this hour and occasion, nobody chooses the full service or the adapted service, because time is limited.

David selects a veggie salad with fresh coconut water, and then looks to everyone. "Let's make good use of the time and thank nature for the good fortune we have in being able to eat. Let's think of all those around us who have the privilege of eating their fill."

The others complete the statement. "May the food be the fuel to our energy."

David exchanges ideas with Bo about India's work force in the southern part of India. Others comment on the subject with their experiences in other parts of the globe. They get a glimpse of how other countries have their own rules and regulations on labour.

Meanwhile, in the adjacent building pertaining to the l'Édifice Vert, Anita is scrolling down the warning list of irregular eating and drinking, as well as leisure habits that might lead to a future health condition directly linked to supply and demand. Through the percentage scale list, Anita analyzes the risk line to see whether it can be adjusted, or whether changes can be made to the risk criteria level, coping with the constant changing and adaptation by ongoing health improvements. Her task is also to advise on the possible dangers and what to do to prevent waste, overuse, or abuse. On the other hand, people have the right to adjust it by themselves or ignore it. But if the condition is imminent, Anita will step in and alter or adapt the foods or drinks they overuse or misuse, by way of changing spices or herbs, or by reducing certain seasonings. Also, friendly advice is given in person through a private screen, showing the benefits of a proper diet that does not exceed the boundaries.

Anita and her team not only watch the intake of food and drinks, but they also watch body temperature, blood pressure, heart rate, and mood swings. The cause of mood swings is inputted into the system and serves as a measure and advice for future incidents.

Anita is assisted by Lindsey and Mark, and they watch over nutrition, physical health, mental health, and human behaviour. In the compound of the l'Édifice Vert, they overlook a crowd of 1,200 fellow members and 4,100 family members.

After lunch, the team members and David leave the purple canteen for their respective quarters. They are anxious for the home coming of Jennifer. Needless to say, they have their fingers firmly on the pulse of any developments in that area.

While David searches the dozen mini-screens on the right-hand side for unexpected anomalies, he watches the centre screens for developments in works in progress. The left screens are for education and innovations. He smiles as he looks to the movements of the STA and the RT77 members. He decides to send a text message to them. "Dear brothers and sisters, stay cool. Know that time is what prevents everything from happening all at once."

Randy glances at his fellow STA team members, each one looking anxiously to the screens and searching for any environmental, political, or hostile signs. He twirls in his chair, drops his head, and tells his team, "This is what you get when you're too efficient. If we were a bit sloppier, we would have more to do than worry."

His colleagues smile, but Eileen is the one to stand up, go over to Randy, and say, "God forbid it would be you to say that something happened to the Benjamin of our main project of the century."

Randy rolls his eyes. "I don't think that even God would deny David this."

Eileen wheels Randy back to his screen while shaking her head. Then she returns to her workspace.

As if to confirm the general mode, a RT77 team member, Rita, pops in and asks the status. They too are going nuts with the waiting game. The digital clock seems to be slowing down, and the turning of the heads of fellow members looks very stiff.

"No danger of capsizing because she is still a thousand miles from the equator," Randy says over his shoulder.

The RT77 member raises a sarcastic eyebrow. "I know the details of her vessel, Randy. You don't have to be annoyed about it."

Randy raises his hands in dramatic surrender. "OK, OK. Nothing funny here. Go back to brooding in your own office." He hasn't finished his sentence before the door is already closed.

Maritime sensors start blinking, and a green blip lets Randy know that the vessel is under the mainland, docking in one of the underground lake ports. He cracks his neck, and while he leaves the internal channel open, he says, "Team, get ready for the reception on my mark."

Chapter 2

The light of the grey door is flickering, and the door opens. Diver Thomas appears in the doorway, still in his diver's suit. With a smile he says, "Voila. This is a quick hello. We are safe and sound, and it's good to be home. Guido and the complete crew will be joining soon." He leaves.

Then comes Jennifer, also in a diver's outfit. She's eager to say hello to the STA and RT77 members. "Hello, guys. I am back. I am still the real Jennifer, so be at ease, and I'll be back in a couple of minutes for the good news. See that there is plenty of sparkling water. See you in a bit." She goes back to the grey door and disappears.

Soon, all STA and RT77 team members gather in front of the purple canteen, making a human tunnel as a welcome reception. David stands as the last member by the canteen door.

It's 1700. The focus is on the successful homecoming of all participants and bringing knowledge to serve a higher purpose. It seems that all are impatiently waiting to discharge this last mission with emotion.

From the entrance comes Guido, and right behind him is Jennifer. Flanked on her left is Thomas, and on her right is Joseph. Suddenly the tunnel of welcome breaks open, and everyone runs towards Guido, Jennifer, Thomas, and Joseph. They hug each other, and tears are flowing, but there are no words.

Discipline is important, but some moments are too important to pass up. Emotions are high during the reunion, and they are taken through a myriad of emotions revolving around coming back home after being away from one's country and family for a long time.

After having hugged and kissed the crew, Jennifer rushes into the arms of David and leans her head against his chest. "It might have taken days," Jennifer said. "Even weeks."

David smiled. "Of course. We are lucky to have good brothers and sisters around. Sometimes they're visible, and sometimes they're invisible. Those we don't know reveal themselves with the sign of the heart – but you knew that, and soon you will get to know them in person."

While she tells the vivid story about escaping and not having the right to show her muscles, they slowly move towards the canteen. In the canteen, the table is set with one glass of water for every member, except for Jennifer, who has one glass of still water and one glass of sparkling water. Needless to say, Anita knows her protégé.

At a sign from David, everyone stops talking and looks to David. "Jennifer, Guido, Thomas, Jo, and all brothers and sisters who are here gathered to welcome the incoming RT77 members. We have valuable earthly information carried by Brian, Rita, Rani, Caio, and Bo, who came in unscathed last week, and today it's Jennifer. Wow, what a gathering we have here tonight. We've got STA Randy, Eileen, Danny, and Ronny. For RT77, there's the DTSC diver team: Guido, Thomas, and Joseph. All are brought together for one cause – our cause. It is undoubtedly an appreciative welcome to you all. Thank you, DTSC Guido, Thomas, and Jo. You have done a wonderful job by piloting all RT77 members safe and sound to their destinations. Thank you, STA members Randy, Eileen, Danny, and Ronny, for your excellent shadow tactics and support. All of you have faced the challenge to survive your determination and give inspiration. The results speak for themselves. Before I hand it over to Anita, Lindsey, and Mark, who will guide and serve you through tonight's bar, I want to say once more: thank you and welcome. It's an immense pleasure and honour to have you here."

David beckons to Anita and her team to take over. A loud applause follows for David, and before Anita can say a word, another round of applause follows for her and her team members.

Anita looks to her right and left. "Boys and girls, this is truly a memorable moment. It's a time to reflect on all the hard work that you have done over the past period. It was not only the hard work but strong team work. All of you have piloted this first phase of the project. It is time to release all the tension and remember that we did what we had to do. There was no right or wrong, and everything went as it should. Only a fool thinks one can change the world; instead, one must work to follow the change towards a smoother future. You all have obeyed the laws of nature and let our strong determination be the energy for us to navigate to the future. Tonight, please follow your hearts and spare your heads for tomorrow. The bar and kitchen are open. Enjoy."

While Anita, Mark, and Lindsey are taking care of everyone, talking to everybody and making sure that happiness and satisfaction rule the game, David quietly leaves the party.

This is the moment where six researchers are reunited after a three-year stay around various parts of the earth. They have analyzed and gathered valuable information on different, diverse, and rich natural phenomena. The next step is to put together all their findings to cross-match and fit them into the puzzle, but that will be for the coming days. The evening slips away, and everyone retires to his or her own nests.

David returns to his place. While he opens the door to his quarter, he looks once more to the dimming lights of the empty hall behind him. It is almost midnight, and when he pushes the door to open, his mind is still with the brothers and sisters he left in the canteen. He says softly, "May the Gods guide you all."

He then walks towards his desk, gives one last glimpse, and sees that all signs are green. He makes a right turn and steps to the bathroom for a cold shower. While he is summarizing the day, he smiles contentedly.

He then slowly steps into the direction of the window of his bedroom, looks to the eastern sky, and says, "Thank you, Lord, for granting me this wonderful day." At a stretch, he hits the bed and in no time is in some dream state, floating high above the mountains overlooking the valleys.

David's biological clock summons him to open his eyes, and he sees daybreak lighting his room He jumps out of bed, goes to the window, greets the sun, and rushes to the bath room. After having refreshed himself, he walks to his desk to consult his daily agenda. The agenda says, "Today is Wednesday, 28 January 2037, the first analytical day of the year 2037. To continue, indicate Yes." David indicates Later and steps away to the breakfast table.

From the touch kitchen, he presses the full service button and then scrolls down to roasted pepper sausage. He asks for two glasses of water and one glass of orange juice. Quickly he pulled another chair to the breakfast table and waits for the food to come.

The bell rings, and a calm and inviting voice says, "Two glasses of water, sir." A hatch swings open, and there are two glasses of water, two serviettes, and one set of cutlery.

David takes the glasses of water and the napkins and cutlery. He places one glass of water with one napkin in front of the chair he has placed by the table. He then takes the other glass of water, napkin, and cutlery and places them neatly in front of him. He looks at the glasses of water, grabs his with his left hand, and holds it to the non-present guest. "May this water raise our energy, wisdom, and peace for today." Having said this, he drinks his water and puts his glass on the table. Next he takes the second glass of water with his right hand and says, "Let this day be productive." He puts the two glasses back in the centre of the table.

As the glasses disappear under the table, the bell rings again. The same calm, inviting voice says, "One glass of cold orange juice, sir." David takes the orange juice, places in front of him, and then pushes the Continue button.

The bell rings, and the inviting voice says, "Two slices of mango covered with some grated lemon peel, a pinch of grated ginger, and a string of honey, sir. Bon appétit." David looks at the two mango bar, neatly sliced. One has the colour of yellowish to orange and lightly sprinkled with grated lemon peel and ginger. The honey string on both sides of the beautifully sliced mango looks yummy.

"Thank you, Lord. I am privileged to have this meal. May the system provide the same to all who aspire to be privileged in life," he says softly. With a gentle gesture, he then picks the little fork with his left hand and the small knife with his right hand, and he consumes it with a smile, leaving nothing on the plate. He places the plate, the fork, and the knife neatly on the tray in the centre of the table.

The hatch closes, and within a minute the bell rings again. The same calm voice says, "Two patties of roasted pepper sausage, made from ground beef and pork, seasoned with minced roasted red pepper, black pepper, salt, fennel, sage, thyme, and oregano. The cooking is done with some coconut oil. The garnish is fresh-sliced tomato and fresh parsley. Bon appétit, sir."

David picks the fork and the knife, looks at them, and says: "No, well." He puts them down, grabs one patty of the roasted pepper sausage with his hand, and takes it to his mouth. After one small bite, he says, "Very delicious and nicely spiced. May everybody who eats this food value and understand the benefit of this healthy sausage." He eats his fill, puts the cutlery on the tray, and pushes the Continue button.

Soon after, the bell rings. The calm voice says, "A glass of fresh fennel tea that comes with the roasted pepper sausage, sir."

David takes the fennel tea from the tray. "This fennel tea must be good for something. I will look into it and add more to my data bank of knowledge." He slowly sips the fennel tea, trying to make the taste his own. "Good taste. I will order it the next time," he mumbles. He then puts the empty glass on the tray.

While he is still trying to understand the taste of the fennel tea, the bell rings again. "This is the last course of the menu: a glass of green smoothie, prepared with half a banana, fresh spinach, wheatgrass, coconut water, almond butter, ice, and a scoop of low-carb chocolate protein. Bon appétit, sir."

David takes the smoothie from the tray, holds it up to look at it, and drinks it in three swigs. He then finishes his orange juice, places the glasses back on the tray, and presses the End button. The bell rings again, and the voice asks David if there is something else needed. He pushes the OK and Thanks buttons.

David stands up, glances at the clock on the wall, and walks towards his desk. He swipes his screen open, and today's agenda reads, "First Analytical Day of 2037." A sweeping motion with his left forefinger on the screen takes him to an intranet page that gives him two choices. The first choice is "Public with ID code", and the second choice is "Admin with ID code". The Public site is accessible to the public in general, with a national ID code. The Admin site is for authorized people, and the authorization is imbedded in the personal ID code. For a second he hesitates about whether to press Public or Admin. He presses Public, and the following advice appears: "You are on a public site. If you wish to continue, press Yes and do not forget to identify yourself with your personal ID. If you want to abort, press No." He presses Yes and identifies himself with his personal ID code. Up comes a renovated home page of this one-day announcement.

Simultaneously, a soft music, instrumental comes with the site, playing "Lara's Theme" from *Doctor Zhivago*, the beautiful "Somewhere My Love", and more from the orchestra of Andre Rieu.

The opening page starts.

> This is your first Analytical Day, Wednesday, 28 January 2037
>
> Good morning, David,
>
> Welcome to the first analytical day of the year 2037.
>
> This first analytical day of the year 2037 is to bring you the latest weal and woe of the community, the whole country, the neighbouring countries, and the world. The idea is to involve and motivate everyone to find and create together for a better result, by giving opinions and suggestions worthy of improving the way of life so that we might lead as an example to the world.
>
> All opinions and or suggestions are given in writing and signed by the author. There is a special box for opinions and suggestions for this special purpose.
>
> The urge is for everybody to create an abstract conceptualization, and to speak up and write to get feedback for better understanding and cooperation. Every analysis and feedback will also be given in writing – as they say, *Verba volant, scripta manent.*

Needless to say, all data and feedback pertaining to the author will be archived in his or her personal data file. This will aid us in exercising and expanding our abilities for automatic analysis and improvement.

The aim is to create responsibility by understanding, where one is to be humbled to have laid the next stone for a wide open and promising future.

We go by the following motto:

We follow, when we have to.
We create, when need to.
We partner, when the time is ripe.

Let us live well today and cheer up for the future.

At the bottom of his homepage, he sees three page links. The left one says Domestic, the middle says Neighbours, and the right one says World.

David decides to visit the Domestic page. It consists of the first page with eight main challenges. After every challenge, there are three columns with numbers. The first column represents the red column, and it means that attention is needed. The second column represents the blue column, and it means that it is under construction. The third column is the green column, and it means that the challenge is effective.

After every main challenge, there is a number in all three columns. This number represents the quantity of sub-challenges in progress.

The eight main Challenges are:

1. Health
2. Relaxation
3. Occupation
4. Education
5. Environment
6. Equality
7. Cooperation
8. War Power

David looks at the quantities of sub-challenges, especially in the red column, which indicates the ones that need attention. The red column of the equality challenge shows the highest number of challenges that need attention. David decides to scroll down and see which sub-challenge from the equality section needs more attention. His fingers go from the top down. He sees Diversity, Culture, Immigration, Emigration, and so on.

Then he stumbles upon the religion challenge. "Hmm, let me check the AFGL on religion, to see how the current guideline is fit together, and how the challenge can affect the AFGL."

David goes through the pages of equality challenge 6000 to find the AFGL pertaining to religion.

AFGL 6055

Religion

1. Religion is strictly private, personal, and unique, cultivating self-mastery and connecting with the creator's vision so as to become naturally creative, avoiding inconsistencies and contradictions.
2. Religion is a belief system in God, the creator of this world and the universe, making known that human beings must protect, maintain, and carry on the creation.
3. Religion can be made public and must be susceptible to questioning, with the aim to achieve higher understanding relevant to the well-being of all living beings on earth.
4. Religion must be made the vehicle to contribute and facilitate the progress of all living beings and their adaptability to understand the ever-changing universe.
5. Religion must give meaning to life, facing reality and taking up responsibility for a safe, honest investigation towards a better life style.

"Let's look at what the challenge is all about." David continues reading to find the root cause.

Red Challenge

Actual Functional Guide line, AFGL 6055 – Religion

- In the most populated communes (such as communes 18, 19, 20, 21, and 22), questions start popping up, even by prominent people, as to why the internationally known Human Rights Act on religion is not prevalent in their communities.

- Foreign scholars well versed in religious matters are willing to come teach for free, bringing the knowledge first hand with original texts and holy books.
- Certain countries are offering financial and logistical aid to bring enlightenment in pressing times. Why trying to reinvent the wheel, when life is short and help is at hand?
- People have the right and freedom of thought, conscience, and religion, as per article 9 of the European Convention on Human Rights, Freedom of Thought, Conscience, Religion, and Non-discrimination.

Possible Consequences and Foreshadowing

- As of date 36.581 (this number is updated daily), people have posted to challenge the Religion AFGL 6055. The expectation is that it can grow to a max of 40.000. The majority of the challengers are of European and African descent.

David frowned and said softly, "I will give it some time to see the feedback come in, as well as how many want to *relever un défi*. By the looks of it, there will be lot to challenge in the coming six months."

After closing the public site, David enters the administrative site. In this site, details of all challenges, authors, and activities related to the author are available; so too are the regions of activities.

In the author page, details of birth, marital status, ethnic origin, previous religious belief, education, and all social, private, and administrative activities are recorded. This page has also a link to genealogical research.

While David is scrolling up and down the author list page, a screen pops up. He looks at the incoming screen, which says that Jennifer is online. He accepts the call, and Jennifer says, "Hey. Anita invited me to lunch and to spend the analytical afternoon with her. Also, she asked me to drag you along. Do not say no, please."

Without hesitation, David replies, "I am in no condition to say no, so I am happy to come. It is now 1200. Pick me up in ten minutes, OK?"

Jennifer says, "Thanks. See you in ten minutes."

David scrolls back to see the other challenges in order to have an overview of other pressing matters. He then closes the screen and gets ready for Anita's.

No door light is flickering, but he hears a special, familiar knock on the door. David has not heard this in three years. He looks at the door screen, though he knows that nobody else has that knock. He opens the door. "Hey. You're a minute early."

Jennifer looks up and says, "No, the distance became shorter than I am used to in Australia."

They hug each other and head to Anita's. It is a three-minute walk through the corridor, one minute in the elevator up, and another minute to Anita's door.

While on the way to Anita's, Jennifer comments, "How nice of Anita to have us over for lunch. I bet that she knows exactly the right timing to talk to us in person."

David nods. "No doubt, my dear. Anita is someone who chooses a word to mean just what she chooses it to mean – not more, not less. But she is an honest and lovely person."

There is no need to knock at the door of Anita, because she spots David and Jennifer on her screen and is already opening the door to welcome her invited guests. With a smile on her face, she welcomes the guests. "Hello, Jennifer, David. How nice that you two could make it. Do come in and make yourself at home while I set the table."

Jennifer hugs and kisses Anita three times on her cheeks, and so does David. Anita once more glances at the screen to see if everything in the corridor is normal. Anita says, "Let us start first with a glass of cold water with a bit of fresh fennel, while we are making our way to the table."

"Hmm, fresh fennel. Where do you get that, Anita?" Jennifer asks.

"I have a chest full of various herbal teas, and another chest with a variety of spices, all freshly plucked and prepared from my own garden. After lunch, I am going to show you my mini BT garden. You are going to love it."

David and Jennifer sit down by the table while Anita is busy finishing some dishes. There are some interesting food stuffs on the table, such as celery sticks, cucumber sticks, some krupuk, and dried rice cakes.

Jennifer's eyes open wide. "This is krupuk, and that is galettes de riz. It reminds me of the biscuits in Australia – the Anzac cookies I used to have on the field. I miss the celery sticks; you could only find them in Japanese restaurants. Hmm, this celery stick is fresh – too fresh in this hot country."

Anita hears this from behind the kitchen balcony and says, "Yes, it comes right from my BT garden." She enters with a tray and takes it to the table. "OK, to begin with, we have sweet potatoes sticks hot from the oven and a dip made with spinach, basil, red pepper, and olive oil. All was prepared in my p-kitchen."

Anita joins David and Jennifer at the table. Anita looks to David and Jennifer, and David signs to Anita to do the honours.

"With love, we prepare the food that the earth brings forth for us to energize our bodies and our will to live. May this food bring us energy and wisdom."

David and Jennifer repeat the last words together. "Energy and wisdom."

After these words, they start to eat. Anita orders from the t-kitchen three glasses of coconut water. The kitchen bell rings, and a tray comes out with three glasses of coconut water. Anita takes the glasses from the tray and puts the drinks on the table.

"Voici, cold coconut water, I know that it is a favourite drink for both of you."

"In the field, we had canned coconut water that was very sweet and originated from Thailand, with the name Pure Young Coconut Water. But in certain places we had fresh coconut water from freshly plucked coconuts."

While they were finishing the sweet potatoes, Anita enters the kitchen and brings three portions of vegetable salad with dressing in a small bowl.

"Hmm. Is it called pecel or gado gado?" asks Jennifer.

"Aha – you remember this!, It is supposed to be gado gado, but it is a mix of both. We have steamed bean sprouts, water spinach, bitter gourd, string beans, steamed cabbage, raw tomatoes, and hard-boiled eggs. This is fried tempeh and fried onions. This is gado gado dressing, made of peanut butter, coconut sugar, dried shrimp paste called terasi, tamarind juice, lime juice, red chilli pepper, some cloves of garlic, diced onion, and water to dilute. All in a food processor, and voila. Bon appetite."

"Thank you, Anita, I think that I understand what you are saying. Now, I am going to use my p-kitchen to have all these fresh and delicious foods, but I'm not used to cooking only for myself. I will do it to experience life in another way."

The food is delicious and light, and they eat without saying a word. Then Anita says, "I love cooking because it is a pleasant diversion. My mind wanders in the agricultural fields and the warungs in Suriname. Those were the happiest times in my youth."

"Tell me about Suriname. How was life at that time? Your school, the food, the environment, and the country," Jennifer says.

David jumps in. "I think that talking about Suriname will take a whole day, and I do not know if this is in Anita's agenda."

"You are right, David. There is so much to tell. The only thing I can tell you today is that we could eat from the trees, roast corn on a fire, and dance on a rice field. We will take a day off soon, and I'll tell you how I experienced life in Suriname." Anita stands up, reaches into the kitchen, and pulls three green plates with some nice snacks. "Jennifer, here is something that you're really going to like it." She sets the plates for the three of them. "We have fried banana as dessert – very light and simple to cook. It's one banana cut into two and enveloped in a mixture of flour, egg, and margarine, with some water to soften it. I use coconut oil to deep-fry it. This is the result, and we eat it warm. Go ahead!"

The fried banana is crispy and golden brown, and it's succulent from the inside. They finish lunch with another glass of coconut water, but this time with coconut pulp.

After the meal, Anita takes David and Jennifer to the balcony. With a hand gesture, the balcony door slides open. Anita points. "Here we are: my pleasant balcony with my tower gardens. On the left is a tower with small growing herbs, and on the right is one with high growing herbs. They have different height in rows. It is a controlled, revolving tower garden. It is programmed for exactly how much sun light is needed, and it turns so that all plants get their share of light. Each tower has a diameter of 60 centimetres and a height of 180 centimetres, divided into 6 columns and 4 rows, which gives me 30 plants on the left tower and 16 plants on the right tower. If the sun light is too hot, sun-blocking glass slides down, protecting the plants against the heat or excessive rain.

"In this tower we have celery on the bottom row. The bottom row is the row where the soil is moisture rich. Celery is known for its richness in vitamins, is low in calories, and helps lower risk for colon cancer, inflammation, and risk of heart disease. It's very useful to treat breast cancer, and the leaves contain the most vitamin C, calcium, and potassium.

"If we look at the back, we have here fennel. Fennel contains vitamins A and C. These antioxidants protect the body from the free radicals. Fennel tea is not only for its aroma; it improves digestion and relieves flatulence and hypertension. For mothers who are breast feeding, it increases milk production.

You can see this one is red beet. The green leaves tell you that it is ripe enough to harvest. The green is very nutritious with nutrients that strengthen the immune system and also support brain and bone health. Beet greens can be sautéed with spinach, water spinach, green beans, or swiss chard. Beet roots contain nutrients that may help lower blood pressure, boost the stamina, detoxify, fight inflammation, and more. One glass of beet juice helps you relax and dilates the blood vessels, improving blood flow and lowering blood pressure.

"I try to have as many plants as possible that are beneficial to our health. In this tower, there are four other plants with a powerhouse of nutrients. In the other tower we have smaller plants of about six different herbs. That one is Moroccan mint, at the back we have pepper mint, and above is banana mint. I keep it small and tidy because mint plants are the most aggressive in the plant world. They spread by runners and by seed.

Everyday mint tea has its benefits. It soothes the stomachs in cases of indigestion or inflammation. The aroma activates the salivary glands, which secrete digestive enzymes to facilitate digestion. It also helps to ease the feeling of nausea and headache, and it has a lot of other practical uses to ease inconveniences. I have here most of the herbs with numerous health benefits."

Jennifer interrupts. "I do not see water spinach."

"Mark occupies a quarter of his balcony to grow water spinach and ginger. He harvests them all year long. Ask him for water spinach or ginger, and he will deliver it right to your kitchen hatch door. There are three others in this compound, Fanny, Gilbert, and Loyd, who grow water spinach or kangkong. You can also find it on the marketplace, where all the surplus goes."

After the balcony tour, Anita takes David and Jennifer to the study, where the screen is on Analytical Day.

Health Challenge

Red Sub-Challenge: Body Mass Index, AFGL 1024

- Period lapse: 12 months
- Threshold exceeded with 2 per cent on average, rate pushed up to 20 per cent for women, 19 per cent for men, 21 per cent for girls, 19 per cent for boys, and 20 per cent for babies.

Alert

- Red Challenge

Possible Consequences and Foreshadowing

- Location: Northern populated areas
- Forecast for 2038: 25 per cent (7 per cent above safety line)

With a sigh, Anita explains, "Due to the economic and commercial deal that's close with the international community, we have conceded the import of food (processed or unprocessed), soft drinks in extract, electronic games, and other electronic items. We have not given specific restrictions on the consumption or the use of them. However, we have issued a hazardous warning of the excessive use of them. Now, the focus of the challenge will be what additional safe counteractions can be taken without stripping off the products that can harm when used excessively."

"So we wait and let the things happen to see where they left the road, and then bring them back on track?" asks Jennifer.

"I would rather say that everyone must exercise free will and learn from their experiences. In the school of life, you will find the best teacher one can get is experience. One can learn and benefit from it, or ignore it and live with the outcome. Nobody may take that away; it is a personal affair. Intervention may only be given with consent, except in extreme cases."

"There may be people who are driven by innocence and achieving things, convinced that it does no harm whatsoever," concludes Jennifer.

"A long ago, someone said, 'When peace has been broken anywhere, the peace of all the countries everywhere is in danger.' Our system has issued the following AFGL on BMI."

AFGL 1024

Body Mass Index (BMI)

1. Internationally accepted BMI also endorsed by the WHO, of which the system is monitoring and adjusts when necessary.

2. BMI safety level:
   a. Yellow – below 18.0 – seek assistance
   b. Desirable – between 18.0 – 25.0 – healthy weight range
   c. Orange – between 25.0 – 30.0 – overweight range
   d. Red – between 30.0 – 40.0 – obese range

3. These BMI measures should not be considered in cases of pregnancy, athletes, and for certain ethnic groups. Specialized advice and a table can be acquired from local healthcare consultants.
4. Your BMI will be monitored, and you will be informed of it, which is part of the General AFGL for Health.
5. Every person is special and unique, and must carry his or her identity with dignity.
6. The system is in place to uphold the dignity by communication advice, and by treating everybody as valid, worthy, and important at a time of vulnerability.
7. The system includes the freedom to act and decide based on mutual understanding.

In the afternoon, David, Anita, and Jennifer discuss how to identify which products, or what parts of products, contain elements to be left out if possible. They also discuss what can be replaced with a healthy, positive alternative in order to change the effect and come to a reasonable and acceptable result. The outcome of this discussion will be couched into a project to be submitted for examination.

After the discussion comes to its end, Anita invites them to go on the balcony. Anita switches the cool blower button to blow cool air on the balcony because even though the sun is going down, it is still hot outside. David and Jennifer stand on the balcony while Anita is in the kitchen.

"Anita, do you need a hand?" asks Jennifer.

"Sure. Can you bring three cold glasses, and fill them with one ice cube apiece?"

Jennifer stands up and goes to the kitchen: "Coming up."

In the meantime, Anita takes cold fennel tea from the fridge and mixes it with some lemon juice and a bit of freshly squeezed sugar cane juice. "Here, you will like this." Anita pours the fennel tea mix into the glasses, and they take the fennel tea to the balcony.

Anita hands out the glasses. "This is a refreshing drink for a hot afternoon."

They enjoy the cold drinks on Anita's balcony, which overlooks the peaceful Approuague River. David talks about the river's history and how, at the time of slavery, the runaway slaves used to hide on the other side of the river.

Anita says, "Talking about slaves, we are going to have a slave dinner. It's a typical African dish, but somewhat modified. We are going to have okra soup with smoked cat fish and tofu."

Jennifer smiles. "Oba – okra soup with smoked fish! I had a feeling that I was going to eat something special that I have not had for years. Thank you, Anita."

"I will need some help, though, so we can finish it in no time."

While Anita puts on some soft music in the background, Jennifer and David stand with a smiles in their eyes, rub their hands, and follow Anita to the kitchen. Anita takes ingredients out of the fridge and puts them on the counter: a bowl with fresh okra, a pack of beef, two red chillies, two ripe tomatoes, some fresh parsley, and a big pack of washed spinach. From the pannier she takes two onions, two cloves of garlic, two bay leaves, and the smoked fish wrapped in recycled paper. From the cupboard comes a bottle of coconut oil, a bottle of olive oil, sea salt, fresh ginger, one bowl, and one skillet.

"David, can you cut the beef in cubes and put them in the skillet on medium-high? When the juice is out, put two table spoons of olive oil, add crushed garlic, and close the lid. Jennifer, please chop the onion, shred the fish, and take out all the fish bones. Open the lid, add the onion and the shredded fish, stir it, add the bay leaves and chillies, and scrape the browned bits on the bottom of the pot. I will add my crushed tomatoes, one and a half litres of water, and the okra which I have cut. David will do the tofu".

After twenty minutes, Anita lifts up the lid, looks at the soup, stirs it, and adds a table spoon of coconut oil, sliced ginger, and salt and pepper. She closes the lid for another twenty minutes. Meanwhile, Jennifer and David get the table ready with the plates and the appropriate cutlery. Anita puts out three glasses of fennel water with a pinch of lemon. She adds some small bottles of beer on the table.

Anita checks the soup and smiles. "Soup is ready, and it looks good, I will bring it to the table."

At the table Anita, she serves the soup and garnishes it with the freshly chopped parsley and the tofu. As usual, Anita gives thanks for the food and for the wonderful help in the kitchen. By their faces of contentment, her guests love the food. For Jennifer, this opens the door for eating a food she loves. She now sees how easy it is to have a variety of healthy foods that are so simple to prepare, especially with some soft music in the background.

After the dinner, they sit for a while, listening to good music, drinking beer, and watching the night sky with its millions of stars flickering important messages to their watchers. After being content with the pleasant, relaxed get-together until late at night, they decide to go home, have a rest, and look forward to the next day.

Thursday, 29 January 2037

After doing the usual morning routine, David is now doing the groundwork for today's meeting, enabling him to understand and pose key questions, as well as make suggestions to come to a measurable outcome. Before leaving his quarters, he looks outside from the eastside window and notices that the sky is dark; a cloud burst is taking place. While looking at the sky, he says softly, "May the rain cool and clean the air above us, stirring up a good mood and fresh ideas upon mankind."

In the hall way while going to the blue door, David bumps up against the janitress, Chloe. Chloe is hasty looking for David. "Good morning, David."

"Good morning, Chloe. What is the rush?"

"It has rained cats and dogs, sir, and I need to see you." Chloe can hardly catch her breath.

"Well, let the cat out of the bag."

"Although there were no anomalies detected, I wanted to make sure that everything is as it should be inside and outside of your place."

He replies, "I have checked and noticed that everything is still standing, but feel free to check. Have a good day, Chloe."

"Thank you, sir. Have good a day."

David thanks her with a smile and continues to the conference room.

The conference lead announces David as chairman of the Environmental Challenge. The cue is given for everyone to take their seats. The project lead commences his introduction.

"Chairman David, today is Thursday, 29 January 2037. Counsellor Jaap will present his advice on Complaints on Cremation AFGL 5033, under the Environmental Challenge."

Counsellor Jaap stands up, holds his hands together, and starts. "Good morning, Chairman. Good morning, members of the committee. There are growing complaints under a certain group of people, mainly from second-generation immigrants, that their deceased loved ones are better remembered and respected when they have an earth and natural burial. Burial will allow the body to decay by a normal process. They argue that it has been a tradition of their ancestors for thousands of years, and this is the best way to help families move from grieving to remembrance. They think that the ashes of their loved ones locked in an urn is inhumane, and that the memorial services better speak to their hearts in their own languages. They also think that the columbaria and the memorial gardens should be more adapted to their personal feelings.

"Chairman David and members of the committee, I see no impediment and found no AFGL that leads to impeding the use of an ancestry language for memorial services. Due to the discrepancy put forward, I have therefore made a script to clarify the pros and cons of Cremation AFGL 5033. Also, in it I have made an approach towards a long-term and sustainable vision of Cremation AFGL 5033 in terms of environmental health, increasing population density, and the dynamics of life. It also emphasizes that every life is worth remembering. I would like to submit it to the committee for examination, and I am happy to discuss it so that we can come to a viable approach to clear the discrepancies."

The committee members look to chairman David and nod positively. Jaap hands out the script to the committee.

Chairman David thanks Jaap for his script and gives a word of assurance that this project will benefit all the people involved. Also, David thanks the committee and urges the committee to do the utmost, together with Jaap, for the benefit of all. After this, David closes the meeting with a toast.

On the way to the canteen, David meets with the Venus Project leader, Winston. The greetings are very warm, and David states he is on the way to the canteen to have a bite. He asks Winston if he wants to join him. Winston says that he was hoping to meet with him.

David says that it is an immense pleasure to have lunch with him. On the way to the canteen, as usual, David inquires about the well-being and progress of the team and the project.

Winston confirms that it is going very well, and everything is set for Saturday. He will close the proposition for phase one on Sunday.

David and Winston enter the canteen and stay for a good hour and a half. They have a good lunch and a nice chat, mostly about personal matters. They say goodbye with a big hug and then exit the cafeteria.

While passing through the courtyard, David stops for a moment to admire the diverse flower culture. *Soon I will have some flowers on my balcony,* he thinks by himself. With a smile, he continues to his office.

Friday, 30 January 2037

When the night meets the dawn, David opens his eyes and watches twilight changing shape, welcoming him to a new day that's balanced with amazing tropical sunshine and rain. As usual, David greets the east with its upcoming sun. He does his morning ritual, which is holy to him, and he does it with full consciousness. When satisfied, he starts the day by examining his agenda.

He swipes his screen open, where today's agenda awaits. "Education challenge: Today's project can be an expansion on AFGL 4017 of Diversity in Education." A sweeping motion with his left forefinger on the screen takes him to the educational diversity challenge.

The project leader is Counsellor Jean-Paul, a professor of the École Centrale du Nord. He will be presenting a new module under the denomination of EAP. Counsellor Jean-Paul is a fervent ideologist. His project is based on current happenings. David looks at Jean-Paul's previous writings, both the latest and the earliest. After that, he closes the screen and gets himself ready for the day.

At the conference room, the conference lead announces David as chairman of the Educational Challenge, and everyone takes a seat. The project lead commences his introduction. "Chairman David, today is Friday, 30 January 2037. Counsellor Jean-Paul will present his project to make an addendum into AFGL 4017 under the heading 'Diversity of the Educational Challenge'."

Before starting with the proposal, Jean-Paul looks a bit nervous, but after a minute of silence, he regains his confidence. "Good morning, Chairman. Good morning, members of the committee. Social media and international political propaganda have revolutionized the way people think, act, and socialize on the web, as well in social gatherings throughout most of the Western world. Social media is becoming a vehicle to rally people for a cause, and it has led to political unrest in many countries. There is cyber bullying, encroaching on personal dignity, and encouraging people to visit websites more often by organizing contests. Those addicted to social media have shifted the focus from the real world.

"Social media is a powerful tool, and so now is the time to create an awareness of human potential on progress and positivity using social media. In order to gain or cover a wide audience, and to be favourably known, we have to start with youngsters – say, at the high school level.

"My project is dealing with people's knowledge – the art of discovering the positive side in human beings. I seek to understand and know the cause of someone who has fallen to a less positive side of life, and I try to find the means to bring this person back on track. I am sure that everybody came into this world with a positive attitude. There is no other way than a 'want to live' attitude. When we observe a new born, we will discover that any newborn, whether from a poor or a rich family and regardless of skin colour, sees the daylight as a new, promising beginning. They show curiosity in their eyes. When they grow older – let say four months – they show a bit of courage to move, no matter how. A few months later, this new born will take the action to do what his or her parents do. What a wonderful thing nature brought us to see.

"We see here the first sequence of actions: curiosity, courage, and action. To make it easy, I combine them and call it Cucourac. We all have this Cucourac within. Our Cucourac is corrupted by the new and so-called modern philosophy of life, which got stuck in the many sideways of explanation defending the incompleteness of the philosophy. Many external forces gain from the incompleteness and indecisiveness, not knowing that they are even forcing themselves to live with it too.

"In order to find a way out of the tunnel, I propose a game to come out in the open. The game is processed in a program or training. I call it EAP, and it starts as a course at the high school level and becomes a module at the university level. EAP stands for Eulogy, Autobiography, and Poetry.

"In Eulogy, or eulogium, we will learn to find the good deed and intention in another person, whether living or deceased. We'll save the good things that can be saved, transform the lesser things into good intentions, and present it in a positive, with words of love and an encouraging scheme.

"In Autobiography, we will experience what can be done, versus what has been done. By having full knowledge of the difference and knowing the similarity from the comparison with eulogy, autobiography will take us to a journey into our past. The more we journey, the more we understand and the more we come to accept the self. The importance here is to come to an honest self-documentation and self-knowledge.

"In Poetry, we will learn the balance of ideas and the connotations that the words carry. It's the art of condensing and compressing the words to convey emotions or ideas, generating a meaning. Poetry will enhance the understanding of eulogy and autobiography, and it will make the stories more memorable and in a more acceptable and loving way. EAP will be enlivened with life sciences and stories correlated with mankind.

"When the three are well investigated, we will come to understand how man's life is interwoven, and how respect can play an important role for the well-being of mankind.

"Using social media to promote the EAP program, creating followers to intertwine with EAP, and discussing the how and the why will undoubtedly create support, particularly the surrealists pushing the rhetoric to its limits. EAP opens the possibility of exploration as a profession, aiding in journalism, politics, and teaching, which can transform any nation to become an explorer of mankind and the universe. "That is why this is very important to start this project with the younger generation, such as students ages from twelve to eighteen. They say what is learned in the cradle is carried to the tomb. I therefore hand this special project to the committee for examination and feedback."

The committee members look to David and nod positively. Counsellor Jean-Paul hands out the project to the committee.

David thanks Jean-Paul for his important work and speaks a word of assurance that this project, together with Jean-Paul's effort, can bring a valuable change in how people interact with each other. Also, David thanks the committee and urges the committee to do the utmost together with Jean-Paul for the benefit of all. After this, David closes the meeting with a toast.

Chapter 3

It is Saturday morning. Precisely at 1000, all RT77 members of the Serving the Cosmic Will group are present in the front chamber, waiting quietly for the announcement of the outer guard.

In the meantime, young apprentices are busy burning candles on the sidewalks, corners, and the middle walk of Conference Room X. In the darkened left (or the north) gallery sit the STA members. In the right (or south) gallery sit the DTSC members, along with HC members Anita, Lindsey, Mark, and the former Chairman Frank.

The presiding officer of Serving the Cosmic Will is the Chairman David. Next to him in official rank is the Venus Project supervisor, Winston, and the two assistant project supervisor, Sue-Ellen and Ben. These officers occupy stations in the east, west, and south, respectively, of Conference Room X, and they're situated due east and west (physically and symbolically) in the symbolism of

Serving the Cosmic Will. They represent the sun at the chairman's rising, his meridian, and his setting. The other officers of Conference Room X are the secretary, senior steward, junior steward, sentinel, and outer guard, and they take rank after the Venus Project supervisors in that order. Also, the apprentices are appointed first and second steward, along with a chaplain and organist. Two stewards sit at the right and left and a little to the front of the first assistant project supervisor.

Upon entering Conference Room X, the first object that typically attracts one's attention is the altar, situated in the centre of the room, midway between east and west and directly opposite south. Near the altar, there are three lights representing the burning tapers of candles, which are situated so as to point towards the east, west, and south. These are always lit before Conference Room X is officially opened. On the altar is a copy of the manifesto. When Conference Room X is opened, the manifesto will have the golden sun placed upon it.

The outer guard prepares the RT77 members, and when he's ready to proceed with the ceremony, he gives three distinct knocks. By giving the knocks with longer intervals, the outer guard indicates that the RT77 members are ready.

The sentinel rises from his chair, takes a step, and gives the sign: "Sister Sue-Ellen, there is a report."

Sister Sue-Ellen is seated. She also gives three knocks, rises, takes a step, and gives a sign: "Chairman, there is report."

The chairman overlooks the room. "Sister Sue-Ellen, inquire who wants admission."

Sister Sue-Ellen asks Brother Sentinel to tell her who seeks admission.

The sentinel goes to the door of Conference Room X, unlocks it, and does not leave the conference room but remains on threshold with a hand on the door handle. He assures himself that members are properly prepared. Says the sentinel to the outer guard, "Whom have you there?"

"Brothers and sisters of RT77 in a state of darkness, who have been well and worthily recommended and properly prepared, and who humbly solicit to be admitted to the mysteries and privileges of Serving the Cosmic Will."

"How do they hope to obtain those privileges?"

The outer guard prompts the RT77 members aloud. "By the help of Mother Nature, being pure, free, and good report," the RT77 members repeat.

"Halt, while I report to sister Sue-Ellen."

The sentinel closes and locks the door, returns to his position in front of his chair, takes step, and makes a sign. "Sister Sue-Ellen, brothers and sisters of RT77 in a state of darkness, who have been well and worthily recommended and properly prepared, and who humbly solicit to be admitted to the mysteries and privileges of Serving the Cosmic Will."

"How do they hope to obtain those privileges?"

"By the help of Mother Nature, being pure, free, and good report."

"The tongue of good report has already been heard in their favour. Do you, Brother Sentinel, vouch that they are properly prepared?"

"I do, Sister Sue-Ellen."

Sue-Ellen reports to the chairman: "Chairman David, there is a good report."

"Then let them be admitted in due form."

Brother Sentinel makes a sign.

Upon seeing this, Chairman David turns to Stewards Fernand and Brother Andre. Both stewards place the stools for the RT77 members in position.

The sentinel takes the poniard and goes to the door, followed by Fernand and Andre. The sentinel opens the door, retaining a hold on it as before. He presents poniard to RT77 brother Brian's left breast. "Do you feel anything?"

After an affirmative answer from Brother Brian, the sentinel raises the poniard above his head to show that he has so presented it.

With his left hand, Brother Andre takes Brother Brian firmly by the right hand. Brother Fernand is on Brother

Brian's left and leads Brian to the stool. All three stand facing east.

After all RT77 members are admitted through the same ritual, The sentinel closes and locks the door, places the poniard on brother Winston's pedestal, and resumes his seat.

The chairman continues. "Brothers and sisters of RT77, as you are aware that no man can be made a servant of Serving the Cosmic Will unless he or she is free and of mature age, I demand of you: are you free and of full age that carries you to the cosmic level?"

Stewards prompt the RT77 members aloud. "I am."

The chairman orders, "Thus assured. I will thank you to kneel while the blessings of heaven are invoked on our proceedings."

Stewards make sure that all RT77 brothers and sisters are seated properly. When things are apparently in readiness, the Chairman raps the gavel, signalling the officers and members to immediately repair to their respective places and take their seats. Before the chairman takes his seat, however, he issues the following command. "The brothers and sisters will be clothed. Officers, repair to their stations and places."

Sister Sue-Ellen sees that the outer guard is at his post, and she asks him if there are brothers and sisters in the front chamber, waiting to enter the CRX. Sue-Ellen then asks the sentinel to fulfil his duty.

The sentinel opens the door without knocking, puts out his head, and whispers to the outer guard, "Who is standing outside the door, that the CRX is about to be opened?"

"Brother Sentinel, there are no other souls in the waiting room."

The sentinel then closes the door and gives three distinct knocks, which are answered by the outer guard in like manner. The sentinel gives one knock and gives a sign to Sue-Ellen.

Sue Ellen faces towards the east and reports, "Chairman David, the CRX is tiled."

"How tiled?"

"By a master servant outer guard, armed with the proper implement of his office."

"The outer guard's station?"

"Outside the inner door, with a drawn sword in his hand."

"His duty?"

"To guard against the approach of cowans and eaves droppers, and to see that none pass or repass but those who are duly qualified and have permission."

"Sister Sue-Ellen, what is the situation of the sentinel?"

"Within the entrance of the CRX."

"His duty?"

"To admit brothers and sister on proof and in due form. Also, to seal up from outer dependency sources like electricity, electronic communications, and the Internet, and to connect with independent sources within Conference Room X."

Sister Sue-Ellen takes her seat, and the chairman gives one rap. "Brother Winston, what is your place?"

"I supervise and guide Project One of Serving the Cosmic Will. Project One is to be delivered within fourteen days, complete with all the parameters, ready with the design documents to manufacture and assemble all components for the go of the Venus Project. Project One is to have all the knowledge to convert Venus's atmosphere into a habitable atmosphere. Projects Two and Three will follow here after."

"You are the guide, then, I presume?"

"I am so taken and accepted among brothers and fellows."

"Brother Winston, what is your secret grip?"

"A certain friendly and brotherly grip, whereby one servant may know another in the dark as well as in the light."

Chairman David proceeds. "Well then, Brother Winston, let us all vouchsafe thine aid, oh Almighty Knowledge and the Supreme Law of the Universe, to our present convention. Grant that these brothers and sisters for Serving the Cosmic Will may dedicate and devote their lives to thy service, so as to become true and faithful servants among us. Endue them with a competency of thy divine wisdom so that, assisted by the little knowledge of Serving the Cosmic Will, they may be better enabled to unfold the beauties of the true wisdom, to the honour and glory of thy cosmic will."

All speak in unison: "I accept and serve the cosmic will."

Chairman David speaks to Winston. "You will call the brothers and sisters to order as servant of Serving the Cosmic Will, reserving yourself for last."

Brother Winston turns to Brother Brian. "What makes you a servant, Brother Brian?"

"My obligation."

"Brother Brian, how do you know yourself to be a servant of Serving the Cosmic Will?"

"I abide by the code of conduct."

"Brother Brian, what is your code of conduct?"

"By having been at first an observer, by trial and error, keeping a just and regular account of the same, and by always invoking the assistance of the great architect of the universe in all my undertakings. May my labour, thus begun in order, be conducted in peace and closed in harmony."

"Brother Brian, enlighten your brothers and sisters of your findings"

"Removing excess heat from the surface of Venus through the process of convection will lower the surface temperature fifty degrees Celsius the first month, and it will gradually lower the temperature in the subsequent months. On sunny days, less dry convection can create rising water vapour to form clouds. Clouds forming under the debris in the troposphere will block the downward infrared radiation, and consequently Venus will lose infrared radiation energy to outer space. This will then create an unstable troposphere, leading to large and intense thunderstorms, producing hail and even tornadoes. When there is enough water vapour producing thunderstorms with hail and rainfall, it may also affect the upper atmosphere, leading to an upper air disturbance. This phenomenon can be found mostly in the Midwest of the United States. For this to happen, we need debris in the troposphere and increased water vapour. Also, in order to bring Venus's atmosphere to a habitable one, carbon dioxide must be consumed, whereby other gasses are to be released. Transforming carbon dioxide into dry ice may accelerate the process. Once the cooling process takes place, bacteria and other protein genes must be introduced, infused, or bombarded into the environment. With the rise of certain gases due to the infusion, the temperature will be cooler, and volcanic eruption hopefully will be less. Consequently, there will be fewer emissions of carbon dioxide into the atmosphere. Brother Winston, this is what I can add for Phase One. Together with other members, I will intertwine the findings to shift to Phase Two."

Brother Winston turns to David.

"Brother David, Brother Brian completed his part in the process and awaits your further indication to proceed."

"Brother Winston, I have taken good notice and see nothing to interfere with the information given. Are you willing to see Brother Brian to his rightful place?"

Winston takes Brian by his left hand and leads him to his seat in the east. Then Winston takes a steps towards Bo. "What makes you a servant, Brother Bo?"

"My obligation."

"Brother Bo, how do you know yourself to be servant of Serving the Cosmic Will?"

"I abide by the code of conduct."

"Brother Bo, what is your code of conduct?"

"By having been at first an observer, by trial and error, keeping a just and regular account of the same, and by always invoking the assistance of the great architect of the universe in all my undertakings. May my labour, thus begun in order, be conducted in peace and closed in harmony."

"Brother Bo, enlighten your brothers and sisters of your findings."

"A cave system is the best first shelter for human, animal, bacteria, and plant. A good cave system is capable of creating its own weather system, having its own fauna and flora system. It also provides protection against severe weather conditions outside the cave. Good and perfect examples of cave living can be found in Vietnam and China. A good one is in China's Shaanxi province, where tens of millions still live in underground homes.

"In the great mountain chain, beginning with Maxwell Mons (which is 11 kilometres high and 870 kilometres long), surely there are caves worthy to explore. To make a cave bigger and deeper, we may make use of tunnel-boring machine drills. The process of implosion might become handy. The soil in the cave must be analyzed for its strength and density, looking for signs of bulging, cracks, the depth of trenches, and the amount of soil moisture. These and all other necessary measures and analyses, such as gravitational forces and environmental conditions, must be taken to prevent cave-ins.

"A Venus reconnaissance drone for the northern hemisphere will shed more light on higher ground, cave entrances, solid landing grounds, gorges, possible riverbeds, and volcanic lakes, as well as tectonic lakes. Mapping Ishtar Terra, the northern continent with its four mountain ranges, will be a good and fast start for terraforming on Venus. As soon as the surface temperature cools down, cave exploration will commence, first by guided floating robots. Brother Winston, this is what I can add for Phase One. Together with other members, I will intertwine the findings to shift to Phase Two."

Winston turns to David. "Brother David, Brother Bo completed his part in the process and awaits your further indication to proceed."

"Brother Winston, I have taken good notice and see nothing to interfere with the information given. Are you willing to see Brother Bo to his rightful place?"

Winston takes Bo by his left hand and leads him to his seat in the east. Then Winston takes steps toward his seat.

Lunchtime approaches, and all brothers and sisters take the necessary steps for a good lunch within the canteen of the CRX compound. Thereafter, they resume their obligation in Conference Room X.

Winston takes steps towards Jennifer.

"What makes you a servant, Sister Jennifer?"

"My obligation."

"Sister Jennifer, how do you know yourself to be servant of Serving the Cosmic Will?"

"I abide by the code of conduct."

"Sister Jennifer, what is your code of conduct?"

"By having been at first an observer, by trial and error, keeping a just and regular account of the same, and by always invoking the assistance of the great architect of the universe in all my undertakings. May my labour, thus begun in order, be conducted in peace and closed in harmony."

"Sister Jennifer, enlighten your brothers and sisters of your findings."

"Under the Australian blue sky, I came to learn that the only thing we have in abundance is light. The light – in this case, the sunlight – is an interesting phenomenon. For example, light affects plants, organisms, and other living beings, even underground or undersea. But most important, it is necessary, and it supports and even creates all life forms known and unknown or yet to be discovered.

"However, when over-exposed to light, especially to UV and other powerful gamma ray particles emitted from solar flares, or X-rays (which is invisible to the naked eye), it becomes extremely dangerous in certain conditions for all life forms. A gamma ray packs at least ten thousand times more energy than a visible light ray. Lying as they do beyond the visible spectrum, gamma rays have no colour and are invisible to the naked eye, but they're detectable with specialized cameras. Gamma rays are the highest energy form of light.

"The rainbow of visible light that we are most familiar with on earth is just part of a far broader spectrum of light, the electromagnetic spectrum. Past the red end of the rainbow, where wavelengths get longer, are infrared rays, microwaves, and radio waves. Beyond violet lie the shorter wavelengths of ultraviolet rays, X-rays, and gamma rays. As we know, rainbows appear when sunlight is refracted into separate colours by water droplets. At the absence of water vapour and clouds, we can diffuse the direct light with a well-polished and shaped diamond cone, bowl, or mirror, with the purpose of reflecting light back to the stratosphere. This causes the positive and negative charge particles to fuse, and with the help of their accompanying waves, we will be creating a stirred layer enough to unblock and scatter the atmosphere so as to ultimately weaken the dense layer and let the hot surface air escape to a higher and cooler layer in the stratosphere. Also, it will give oxygen the chance to separate itself from carbon dioxide and eventually join with the existing ozone, making the layer thicker and denser. This will lead to a cooler troposphere, and consequently a cooler temperature on the surface. The cooler temperature creates condensation, and consequently water vapour creates water droplets. If the process is successful, a rainbow will appear in the sky.

"To help speed up the cooling process, cultivating cyanobacteria in various parts of a hot continent is the most effective and the natural way to consume carbon dioxide and deliver oxygen to the surface. By approximation, one square meter of blue-green algae can produce significant oxygen every day, which is necessary for creating a breathable atmosphere on Venus. Cyanobacteria are photosynthetic and heat resistant, and they can produce their own food. Biostromes can and will be formed when there is enough condensed water produced from the process of cooling the temperature. With the available water, the algae will rapidly expand. Also, note that water is a chemical reductant of cyanobacteria. Examples of cyanobacteria forming biostromes of several meters thick and many kilometres wide and long can be found in the Shark Bay at the Gascoyne Region, West Australia. Cyanobacteria are important organisms for the health and growth of many plants. Algae and cyanobacteria may release nitrogen gas to form new nutrients that are beneficial and keep the nutrient cycle going.

"Together with cyanobacteria, it is also good to export lichen, which is a type of symbiotic organism made up of a plant-like partner and a fungus. Individual lichen is composed of a mycobiont, or fungus, combined with a photobiont or phycobiont in the form of green algae or cyanobacteria. The algae or bacteria photosynthesize, providing nutrients for the fungus and giving the lichen its characteristic greenish or bluish colour.

In a joint effort with the evolution of fungi, plants will be created. The percentage of oxygen will increase, and the level of carbon dioxide will decrease, lowering Venus's surface temperature. Brother Winston, this is what I can add for Phase One. Together with other members, I will intertwine the findings to shift to Phase Two."

Winston turns to David. "Brother David, Sister Jennifer has completed her part in the process and awaits your further indication to proceed."

"Brother Winston, I have taken good notice and see nothing to interfere with the information given. Are you willing to see Sister Jennifer to her rightful place?"

Winston takes Jennifer by her left hand and leads her to her seat in the east. Then Winston takes steps towards Caio. "What makes you a servant, Brother Caio?"

"My obligation."

"Brother Caio, how do you know yourself to be servant of Serving the Cosmic Will?"

"I abide by the code of conduct."

"Brother Caio, what is your code of conduct?"

"By having been at first an observer, by trial and error, keeping a just and regular account of the same, and by always invoking the assistance of the great architect of the universe in all my undertakings. May my labour, thus begun in order, be conducted in peace and closed in harmony."

"Brother Caio, enlighten your brothers and sisters of your findings."

"From all the plants and trees, there is one important tree which I have observed: the tipuana tree, better known as the rosewood tree. This plant is a drought-resistant plant, and it can survive under extreme weather conditions and in nutrient-deficient soils, because of the nitrogen-fixing bacteria and fungi in its roots. It grows up to thirty meters high and can have a width of twenty meters, and it is favoured as a shade tree. It has an enormous spreading capacity due to its prolific seeding of some eight thousand seeds per plant. Wind carries the seeds to widely establish them. The different types of rosewood are the Brazilian rosewood, the Indian rosewood, and the Madagascar rosewood. In Brazil, the rosewood in on the verge of extinction – not because of illegal logging, but because the seeds of the few remaining trees are consumed by rodents. Dozens of bags with these seeds – let's say some ten thousand seeds each – an cover a significant area when fully grown, with shade to further cool the area, not to mention the absorption of carbon dioxide.

"Furthermore, we have experimented with satisfaction in creating drought-tolerant plants in the desert of Pernambuco. We have planted chickpea, tepary bean, moth bean, rice, tomatoes, and cassava on the riverbanks of the Sao Francisco River. We then move bit by bit from the riverbank towards the sertão and plant the same plants with less water, until we find out how to treat the plant to adapt itself while still having the same result. Today, we can grow a plant without water from the soil, but only with some humidity in the air and under a ventilated, coloured cover or shelter.

"Also, we have identified some insects (like bees) that are useful for pollinating certain plants.

Now, when the temperature on Venus drops to an acceptable level, we will have the plants do their share on the surface. Brother Winston, this is what I can add for Phase One. Together with other members, I will intertwine the findings to shift to Phase Two."

Winston turns to David. "Brother David, Brother Caio has completed his part in the process and awaits your further indication to proceed."

"Brother Winston, I have taken good notice and see nothing to interfere with the information given. Are you willing to see Brother Caio to his rightful place?"

Then Winston takes steps towards Rani. "What makes you a servant, Sister Rani?"

"My obligation."

"Sister Rani, how do you know yourself to be servant of Serving the Cosmic Will?"

"I abide by the code of conduct."

"Sister Rani, what is your code of conduct?"

"By having been at first an observer, by trial and error, keeping a just and regular account of the same, and by always invoking the assistance of the great architect of the universe in all my undertakings. May my labour, thus begun in order, be conducted in peace and closed in harmony."

"Sister Rani, enlighten your brothers and sisters of your findings."

"I have studied how fish swim in shallow and deep waters. Whether big or small, all fish use fins to move forward, change directions, keeps upward position, and stop. Some bigger fish move through the water using their tail fins. Others use pectoral fins for balancing, steering, stopping, and regulating their speed. The pectoral fins are located behind the gills of a fish, and they come in pairs. In flying fish, the pectoral fins enable the ability to maintain flight. Pectoral fins work much the way the wings of a bird or an airplane do. Also, it is good to know that the tail fin lifts the back of the fish, and the pectoral fins lift the front. The tail fin is called the caudal fin, and if it is used to do the propulsion, the pectoral fins are used to maximize its manoeuvrability. A dorsal fin is a fin located on the backs of most fish. Dorsal fins enable sharks and other fish species to remain upright as they swim through the water. Most of the time, sailfish and billfish keep their dorsal fin retracted.

"The paired pelvic fins or ventral fins are located below and behind the pectoral fins. The pelvic fin assists the fish in going up or down through the water, turning sharply, and stopping quickly. Birds use the same principle to move from one point to another. So do bees and flies in open air. Fish in denser water need short fins in relation to their body size. Birds in thin air within the earth's atmosphere need longer wings and tails in relation to their body size, to be able to have flexible movement.

"With this knowledge, we can calculate the wing and tail size to be mounted on a comet or a planetoid. Changing direction will be coordinated from the ground. Also, a propulsion engine is needed to aid in changing or correcting direction. Calculation and design will be adapted according to the comet or planetoid, as well the propulsion engine. Speed of the comet and distance will be taken in account. Brother Winston, this is what I can add for Phase One. Together with other members, I will intertwine the findings to shift to Phase Two."

Winston turns to David. "Brother David, Sister Rani completed her part in the process and awaits your further indication to proceed."

"Brother Winston, I have taken good notice and see nothing to interfere with the information given. Are you willing to see Sister Rani to her rightful place?"

Winston takes Rani by her left hand and leads her to her seat in the east. Then Winston takes steps towards his seat. As dinnertime is approaching, the sign is given, and the members make their way to the canteen of the CRX. After dinner, they talk about the experiences till bedtime.

On Sunday morning, everybody is ready for the group rituals. After a pleasant and refreshing ritual, they resume their work. Winston takes steps toward Rita. "What makes you a servant, Sister Rita?"

"My obligation."

"Sister Rita, how do you know yourselves to be servant of Serving the Cosmic Will?"

"I abide by the code of conduct."

"Sister Rita, what is your code of conduct?"

"By having been and at first an observer, by trial and error, keeping a just and regular account of the same, and by always invoking the assistance of the great architect of the universe in all my undertakings. May my labour, thus begun in order, be conducted in peace and closed in harmony."

"Sister Rita, enlighten your brothers and sisters of your findings."

"Ever since the Hubble telescope started transmitting pictures and information, we have compared it with other reconnaissance information. I can say in all confidence that within the main asteroid belt, we have all the tools and materials needed to bring the terraforming of Venus closer to realization. Within the main asteroid belt and among the billions of asteroids, or planetoids if you wish, are dozens of small, ice-carrying planets with an iron core. Most of them are half to three-quarters the size of our moon. Because they are travelling within the main asteroid belt, which is shepherded by the sun's gravitational forces, we will be able to harvest three of them and toss them at Venus. We can use them while the time is ripe; if we do not, then we will enter into a situation of 'use it or lose it'. The first harvest will be two of them. These two, one after the other with a time lapse of 180 seconds, must precisely hit the mountainous south pole. This will cause a gentle start to increase the rotation of the planet Venus. The impact of these two icy planets with an iron core on Venus, which are placed and timed correctly and taking into account that these little planet travel at a speed of 85,000 kilometres per hour, will create huge debris in the atmosphere.

"The third icy planet, also with an iron core, will be placed and timed correctly to meet the upward blast enough for the third planet to sling up, and while it is shot up, it slightly changes course and moves upward. Upon coming back, this third one is minutes away on the same route. It will not hit Venus as the two before it, but on its way, it will take up the debris, which will slow it down enough to bring it into an elliptical orbit around Venus. The third planet's momentum and the gravitational force of Venus must be balanced to hold this planetoid in orbit, giving the gravity and tidal forces of the planet Venus enough time for it to function as a moon. The tidal forces are new and irregular in behaviour, and so the distance between the moon and Venus must leave enough room and the flexibility to not invade the Roche Limit, as calculated by French mathematician Edouard Roche.

"There will still be enough debris in the atmosphere, which will function to block the sunlight and hold back the solar winds, resulting in cooling down the temperature and creating condensation, giving time to form ice on the surface of Venus. The newly created moon will clear the debris through its orbit, and gravity forces will slowly clear the debris from the atmosphere, making space for the sunlight to thaw out the ice. The expectation is that the sun creates a torrid zone, sending the cold water vapour to the newly created south and north poles. At the same time, with enough iron on the surface of Venus, a magnetic field will be formed between these newly created poles. Together with the thickening of the ozone layer, solar winds and severe gamma rays will be deviated to outer space. With this in place, temperature will be cooled down to an acceptable level, the atmospheric pressure on the surface will become more earth-like. Condensation will do its job, creating humidity that rises above the surface and forms clouds, which will fall like rain from the sky, clearing up the sulphuric acid in the atmosphere. Meanwhile, the water vapour pushed to the poles, along with the faster rotation of Venus, means ice caps can be formed at the poles. The moon orbiting

Venus will function as the climate regulator for Venus, and it will also stabilize the spin and tilt of the planet. While Venus's atmosphere is cooling down, the rotation increases. Hopefully the moon can function as a shield, attracting the meteors that hit the planet Venus every once in a while."

Sister Rita pauses for a minute, watches the silence in the room, and then continues. "Brother Winston, with all these information at hand, I may say that this completes Phase One. Together we will upgrade this project of Serving the Cosmic Will to Phase Two. We all are looking forward to bringing Phase Two into action"

After Rita says this, Winston turns to David. "Brother David, Sister Rita completed her part in the process and awaits your further indication to proceed."

"Brother Winston, I have taken good notice and see nothing to interfere with the information given. Are you willing to see Sister Rita to her rightful place?"

Winston takes Rita by her left hand and leads her to her seat in the east. Then Winston takes steps towards his seat. After a moment of silence, David and Winston lay out the steps to be taken to complete Phase Two of Serving the Cosmic Will. All members vouch to bring Phase Two quickly to execution. David then ceremoniously closes the meeting.

And with this, we close part one.

Senir Wongsokerto

The Meanings of Foreign Words

au boulot: back to work

Bandung: city in Indonesia

ce qui est bien: this is good stuff

délicieux: delicious

gado gado: mixed vegetables dish

galettes de riz: rice cakes

itu bagus: this is good stuff

l'Édifice Vert: the Green Building

pecel: mixed vegetables dish

pronto: ready

relever le défi: take up the challenge

revenir à soi: meditation

santé: health

sertão: Brazilian dessert

tempeh: soybean cake

terasi: shrimp paste

tufu: cheese-like soy curd

Verba volant, scripta manent: Words fly away, writings
remain

voici: here we go

voila: here it is

warungs: small eating establishment

Abbreviations and Acronyms

AFGL: actual functional guidelines

CRX: Conference Room X

Cucourac: Curiosity, Courage, and Action

DTSC: Diver Team of the Southern Continents

EAP: Eulogy, Autobiography, and Poetry

HC: health care

HK: Hong Kong

Jaka: Jakarta, a city in Indonesia

P-kitchen: private kitchen

RT-77: Research Team 77

STA: Support Team A

Team SC: Team for the Southern Continents

T-kitchen: touch kitchen

Printed in the United States
By Bookmasters